THE TWO OF THEM

THE TWO OF THEM

WRITTEN AND ILLUSTRATED BY **ALIKI**

MULBERRY BOOKS • New York

Published by Greenwillow Books, a Division of William Morrow & Company, Inc., 1350 Avenue of the Americas, New York, NY 10019.   Printed in Hong Kong.   First Mulberry Edition, 1987
10   9   8

Library of Congress Cataloging in Publication Data: Aliki.   The two of them.
Summary: Describes the relationship of a grandfather and his granddaughter from her birth to his death. [1. Grandfathers—Fiction.   2. Death—Fiction] I. Title. PZ7K.A397Tw [E] 79-10161
ISBN 0-688-07337-9

For those who remember

The day she was born,
her grandfather made her a ring
of silver and a polished stone,
because he loved her already.
Someday it would fit her finger.

He made a bed her size
and covered her
with a rosebud blanket
to keep her warm,
and sang her lullabies
she did not yet understand.

He brought her food from his store
to help her grow
and caught her before she fell
when she took her first steps.

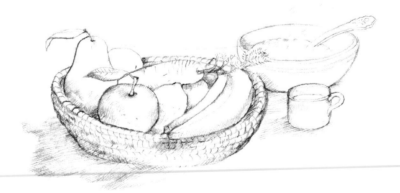

In summer they swam in the ocean
and collected shells together,
and her grandfather watched
from under the shade of a big umbrella
as she made a castle in the sand.

Sometimes
they went to the mountains
and walked in the woods,
and she floated down the creek
on a rubber tire.

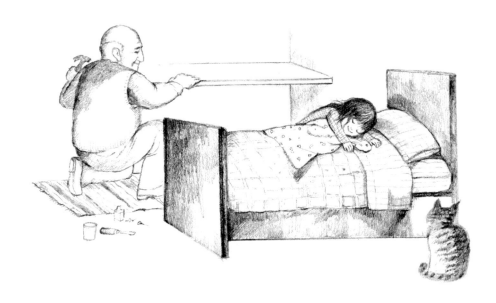

When her bed was too small,
her grandfather made another
for her to grow into,
and a shelf for the books
she would read,
and a doll to hold.

He sang her songs,
and told her stories of long ago
that had been told to him.
Some he made up,
and some were about his love
for the little girl.

She helped him in his store after school,
and loved the smell of the sawdust
he sprinkled on the floor when it rained.

Sometimes she gave out the wrong change,
but at lunchtime,
when they ate their hot soup,
he laughed about it,
because she was just learning to count.

Then her grandfather gave up his store
and grew fruit in his garden instead.
They picked apples and plums and tomatoes,
and there was more time.

He made a cradle for her doll,
and a flute of bamboo,
and they sat under the trees
and played music together.

And every year she loved him even more
than the things he made for her.

Time passed,
and the ring fit the little girl's finger,
and it seemed, suddenly,
that grandfather was an old man.
One night he became ill,
and after that,
part of him could not move.

The girl wheeled him in his garden,
and cut apples for him to eat
and saw that his cup was full.

At night she tucked him in bed
and sang to him
and told him stories he had told her.
Some she made up,
and some were about hot soup,
and sand castles,
and floating in the cool water
on a rubber tire,
and of her love for him.
She said, "Good night, Papouli,"
and he answered with a kiss.

She knew that one day he would die.
But when he did,
she was not ready,
and she hurt inside and out.

It was spring,
and she cut blossoms from his trees
and gave them to him,
and said, "Good night forever, Papouli,"
but he did not answer.

The blossoms became apples
which hung unpicked on the tree.

She picked them,
knowing he would not want them
to fall and rot.

She thought of the tree,
once bare, then in blossom,
and now bearing fruit for her to pick.
The tree would change with the seasons,
again and again.

She would be there
to watch it grow,
to pick the fruit,
and to remember.

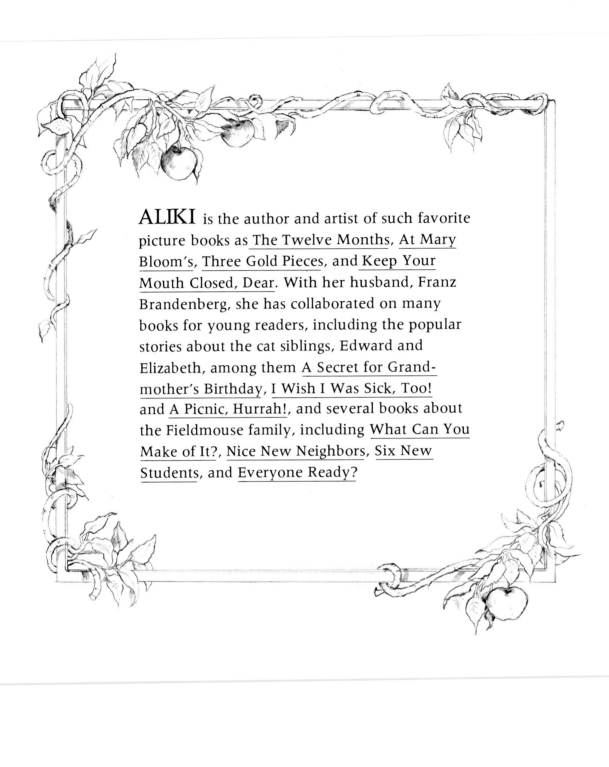

ALIKI is the author and artist of such favorite picture books as The Twelve Months, At Mary Bloom's, Three Gold Pieces, and Keep Your Mouth Closed, Dear. With her husband, Franz Brandenberg, she has collaborated on many books for young readers, including the popular stories about the cat siblings, Edward and Elizabeth, among them A Secret for Grandmother's Birthday, I Wish I Was Sick, Too! and A Picnic, Hurrah!, and several books about the Fieldmouse family, including What Can You Make of It?, Nice New Neighbors, Six New Students, and Everyone Ready?